GREAT
GRANDPA'S
HOUSE

To get there she had to go in a train, then across the sea in a ferryboat, then by car along a winding road for a long, long time. When she got there she was so tired she went straight to sleep. It was in the morning that she first heard the reed pipe.

"You won't be lonely," Keiko's Papa and Mamma had told her. "Your little cousin Yôji will be there."

"I don't like my little cousin Yôji," said Keiko who had never met him.

A Red Fox Book

Published by Random House Children's Books
20 Vauxhall Bridge Road, London SW1V 2SA

A division of Random House UK Ltd
London   Melbourne   Sydney   Auckland
Johannesburg and agencies throughout the world

1 3 5 7 9 10 8 6 4 2

First published in Great Britain by Julia MacRae 1992

Red Fox edition 1994

Printed in China

RANDOM HOUSE UK Limited Reg. No. 954009

ISBN 0 09 925491 3

GREAT GRANDFATHER'S HOUSE

Rumer Godden

Illustrated by Valerie Littlewood

Red Fox

For Akiko
with grateful thanks

Tsui siisi kala sichipii!

"I don't like Great Grandfather's house," said Keiko. "How do you know?" asked Yôji. "You haven't been here yet."

* * * *

'Sayonara' is the Japanese word for 'goodbye'; last night Keiko had said goodbye to her Papa and Mamma and cried herself to sleep. Now she was woken by sounds she had never heard before: the flip-flop of Great Grandfather's old-fashioned sandals on the stone paths of the garden, the tapping of his stick; a "chk chk chk," Old Mother calling her hens to be fed; a heavy chop-slow-chop as Gen-san the handyman chopped wood for the stoves. Then came a piping – she did not know it was from a little reed pipe played by someone – and a small head came round her screen door. "Time to get up, Keiko."

Keiko was a little Japanese girl who had lived in the city all her life so that her cheeks were pale; she wore her black hair in a pony tail held by a band with scarlet beads. Her eyes were black and bright; she would have had a pretty mouth if it had not so often been pouting. She was big and strong and quick ("Too quick," said Papa) and always got her own way until, "We are going to England," Papa and Mamma told her – England is very far from Japan. "We can't take you with us so we are sending you to spend three months with Great Grandfather and Old Mother in the country."

"I won't go," said Keiko and she slapped their hands away, kicked the furniture and cried.

"Perhaps Old Mother will teach you some manners," said Papa.

"I don't want any manners," sobbed Keiko.

"Manners," Old Mother was to say, "are like the oil put into engines to make their wheels go round without trouble, otherwise they jar and grind, grrh, grrh, grrh, grrh."

There were a great many grrhs at first for Keiko in Great Grandfather's house.

To get there she had to go in a train, then across the sea in a ferryboat, then by car along a winding road for a long, long time. When she got there she was so tired she went straight to sleep. It was in the morning that she first heard the reed pipe.

"You won't be lonely," Keiko's Papa and Mamma had told her. "Your little cousin Yôji will be there."

"I don't like my little cousin Yôji," said Keiko who had never met him.

She met him now. Keiko was seven, Yôji was six, but he was such a small boy he looked more like a four-year-old, with a snub nose, black hair cut in a fringe and big dark eyes that were as quick as a moth's antennae.

"You *are* little!" Keiko said as soon as she saw him.

"I'm big enough for me," said Yôji, and he said like a grown-up, "Welcome to Great Grandfather's house. I come every year."

"I don't like Great Grandfather's house."

It was then that Yôji said, "How do you know? You haven't been here yet."

* * * *

Great Grandfather's house was not at all like Keiko's house in the city, among hundreds of others all alike as toy bricks and close together. Great Grandfather's house was long and low with a roof of old tiles, a porch verandah and small rooms divided by paper screens that slid; cream-coloured matting was on the room floors. "No carpets!" said Keiko. There were cushions to sit on. "No chairs," said Keiko. The tables were

low. The biggest room had an alcove, a holy place, where Old Mother liked to put a special vase of flowers and the best of Great Grandfather's paintings. The house felt warm and lively with Old Mother's kettle steaming on the stove all day in the kitchen.

Round the house was the garden with a stream running into a pool that had a little bridge. There was a big stone lantern where Old Mother liked to put a light at night. At the gate was a maple tree; now, as it was autumn, its leaves were as scarlet as the band in Keiko's hair. There was a little wood, a spinney, with an old oak tree and lucky pine trees.

* * * *

Old Mother showed Keiko the drawers for her

clothes in her room. "You must keep them tidy."

"I?" asked Keiko in suprise.

"Who else?" said Old Mother.

"I, *myself?*"

"Of course."

"I don't like Old Mother," Keiko told Yôji, "or Great Grandfather."

Great Grandfather was a tall old man with wispy white hair and a white beard but Old Mother was round and plump, her face crinkled like a walnut; it crinkled more when she laughed. They both wore kimonos and white tabi-socks that had a separate big toe. When they went outside they wore sandals. "Nobody wears those nowadays," said Keiko.

"We do," said Great Grandfather. "We like the old ways."

"I like everything new," said Keiko and she told Yôji, "You should throw your old panda away and get a new one."

"Throw – Panda – *away!*" Yôji was shocked. To him his toy panda was the best panda in the world.

Yôji was a silent little boy except when he was piping; it was a little reed pipe Gen-san had made for him.

"But why don't you talk?" chatterbox Keiko asked Yôji.

"I can't talk," said Yôji. "I'm listening."

"Listening to what?"

"Sough, sough, that's the wind in the maple tree." Now Yôji had begun to talk, the words came tumbling out. "Ssrh, ssrh, those are the bamboos. Gurgle, gurgle, that's the stream.

Scritch, scritch, that's Old Mother's hens. Tsui bii
bii, that's my titmouse."

"What's a titmouse?"

"A little tiny bird as small as a mouse. He's not all
black and white, like most tits, he's got colours on
him. I don't know where he comes from, but if I
play my pipe, he pipes too, Tsui bii bii."

"I don't hear anything," said Keiko.

"That's because you're such a noisy little
person!" Old Mother had come in."If you want
to hear, you have to be quiet like Yôji."

Keiko put out her tongue at Yôji and ran away
into the garden. All the same, in the garden she
was suddenly quiet. She did not thomp with her
feet because she was standing still; she did not
chatter because there was no-one to talk to; and,
"Sough, sough," went the wind in the maple tree,

Sough ~ Sough ~

a red leaf came spinning down. "Ssrh, ssrh," the bamboos were stirring. "Gurgle, gurgle," that was the stream with a little splash when it met a stone. It was as if all of them were talking. "Scritch, scritch," Keiko saw Old Mother's hens, four brown hens, two white and a cock with a red crest and a glossy tail. "Bii bii," she heard like the smallest piping. There were other birds, of course, but this one came near; "Tsui bii bii,"piped Yôji's titmouse and she caught a flitting speck of colour.

Keiko was not only listening, she was looking.

* * * *

The first grhh came that very same morning.

"Children," said Old Mother, "would you like to come with me to collect the eggs?"

"I collected them yesterday," Yôji was proud.

"Then Keiko can collect them today."

Keiko had only seen eggs in shops. Now, in the hen house at the bottom of the garden, the straw was still warm in the nesting boxes and, in each, on the straw was an egg, brown, clean and shining. A big white hen was still sitting; when she saw the children she got off the nest with a squawk and there was another egg.

Keiko gasped.

"Here's the basket," said Old Mother, "put them in one by one," then, "*carefully*, Keiko."

She was too late. Keiko had grabbed the basket, grabbed an egg in her hard little hand and it broke, splattering her with yellow and slimy white over her hand and coat and shoes.

"Wah!" cried Old Mother.

"Wah! wah!" cried Keiko.

Great Grandfather was a famous artist. In spring he painted plum blossom; in summer he painted peonies and butterflies; in autumn he painted the maple tree's red leaves; sometimes he painted people. He had a painting room with his painting things spread on the floor where he worked, sitting on a cushion. There were jars of water, tubes, bottles and small bowls for paint and inks; a little stand held brushes hung by loops – one brush was fine as a whisker. He had a palette for mixing his paints. "You can go in," Old Mother told the children, "but you mustn't touch."

Keiko touched. She took a paint brush off the stand – it was the one as fine as a whisker – and upset a jar of water; a bowl of red paint was sent spinning across the matting making a pool.

Keiko was aghast.

"Little girl!" said Great Grandfather sternly, "if I were a proper Great Grandfather I should tie your hands behind you."

Keiko was more aghast.

"As I am not that kind of Great Grandfather," said Great Grandfather, "you can go outside at once. *At once!*" said Great Grandfather.

Keiko went like a very small snail.

"I'll go too," said Yôji.

* * * *

"It's a lovely day." said Old Mother. "Why don't you two go out and play?"

"What shall we play with?" asked Keiko.

She had brought two large suitcases besides her transistor which she carried. One of the

suitcases was full of toys; she had dolls, a doll's tea-set, a dressing table set, a tiny cooking stove with pots and pans, an electric toy sewing machine, a toy owl, every sort of game and a little toy dog that turned somersaults. Her room next to Yôji was full.

Yôji's was almost empty. He had brought one bag. His only toys were his panda who slept with him – it had lost one ear – and a paper kite with a dragon painted by Great Grandfather. "When I fly it I can feel the sky," he said.

"Is that all you've got?" asked Keiko. "How can you play?"

"Come and see."

"See what?"

"My boats."

"You haven't got any boats," but Yôji led the

way to the stream.

Titmouse came too, "Tsui bii bii." Keiko had never seen such a tiny and cheeky bird with white on his face, a black head, coloured wings, and the brightest of beady black eyes.

Yôji had made a little harbour of stones; three barge boats were there, chips of wood with a nail in them so that they could be tied to a twig with a thread of cotton. They were loaded with gravel and toadstools.

"They float beautifully," said Yôji. "See," he untied one and, true, it floated down the stream to the pool where it turned round and round.

"They're my barge boats," said Yôji. "These are my little ones."

There was a fleet of sailing boats in the harbour, each one a half of a walnut shell with a

match stick for a mast and a postage stamp for a sail.

"Where did you get them?"

"Great Grandfather made them for me."

"Great Grandfather!" Keiko couldn't believe it.

"After I showed him how. No, he showed me," Yôji had to admit.

"But ... You don't make toys. You buy them."

"You couldn't buy these," said Yôji.

That was true. The walnut shell boats bobbed on the water like real boats. "This one is mine," said Yôji. It had a blue stamp sail. "This red one is yours. We'll put them in the stream and they'll race to the pool."

Keiko seized her boat, put it crooked on the water and gave it such a hard push that it went under. "No! No!" cried Yôji. "Use your finger

and thumb and put it in gently." The next one turned topsy turvy. "*Gently,*" said Yôji, and this time it, another red one, started and sailed. Keiko was wild with excitement.

Sometimes the two little boats met an eddy and turned round and round; sometimes they hit a stone which was like a rock to them but the stream carried them on and Keiko began to love her boat with the red sail. Nearer the pool the boats went faster. The children had to run until, "I've won!" cried Keiko but she hadn't, the boat with the blue sail was far across the pool.

"*I've* won," said Yôji.

Keiko was furious. "I won't play anymore." Yôji did not hear. He was back at his harbour.

Keiko fetched her transistor, a doll and the little dog who turned somersaults but the

transistor seemed to play much the same tunes, the doll sat and stared while the little dog's somersaults were always the same. Keiko seemed to see the little boats flashing in the stream, the chip wood barges floating with their toadstool and gravel cargoes, and she went back to Yôji. "I'll play now," but Yôji was not playing boats any longer.

"What are you playing?"

"Bamboo horses," said Yôji.

"How can bamboos be horses?"

"Easily," said Yôji. "Bamboos are much better. Gen-san cut them for me."

"Who's Gen-san?"

"He works here. He's my friend." Keiko had seen the big smiling young man who followed Great Grandfather everywhere. She was beginning to be jealous when Yôji said, "Gen-san can cut a bamboo horse for you too."

"For *me?*"

"Yes, come and try."

The bamboo canes were slim; they bent and rose between their legs. Gen-san had shaped the bamboo's leaves into manes and tails that swished as the children galloped. Titmouse flew from bush to bush piping in excitement. Keiko was soon out of breath. Her cheeks were red and she laughed as she did not often laugh when she was playing.

* * * *

For midday dinner they knelt on cushions around a low table though Great Grandfather sat cross-legged; each had a pair of chopsticks – Keiko's and Yôji's the right size for a child.

Old Mother carried in a tray of steaming small

bowls. She had made a special dinner: mixed rice with vegetables with cooked seaweed, Japanese omelette thinly sliced and fish fried crisp.

It was good; Keiko gobbled so quickly that her chopsticks made a clatter in her bowl. Great Grandfather raised his eyebrows in surprise.

"Keiko, not so quickly."

Keiko still gobbled, sometimes she stuffed her mouth with her fingers.

"Keiko!" And Great Grandfather said, "Clatter, clatter. Shovel. Chomp. Chomp. Eat nicely like Yôji."

Keiko went bright red. She did not dare answer Great Grandfather but, holding her chopsticks in her left hand, with her right she gave Yôji's cushion such a pull that it toppled him over; his head bumped the floor so hard that tears came into his eyes.

The tears did not fall. Like a true Japanese boy, Yôji sat up again on his cushion, picked up his chopsticks and went on eating, but Old Mother stood up as Great Grandfather said, "Old Mother, I will not have roughness and rudeness in my dining room. Please send Keiko to her room."

* * * *

Keiko had never been sent to her room before. After five minutes she called to Old Mother, "Can I come out now? "

"Great Grandfather says 'No'." When Great Grandfather said 'No' , it meant 'No'.

"You mean I have to stay here?"

"Great Grandfather says 'Yes'." When Great

Grandfather said 'Yes', it meant 'Yes'.

Keiko began to cry.

There was a little tune played on a pipe, then a tapping on the paper screen wall and a whisper, "Keiko."

"Yôji! Where are you?"

"In my room."

"But you weren't sent there."

"If you were sent I wanted to be. Keiko, I'll tell you my new secret. I've got a toad."

"What's a toad?"

"He's like a special kind of frog," but Keiko had never seen a frog either.

"Look, I'll put him through."

Keiko was going to say 'No' but Yôji had managed to slide the wall back and Toad was on the floor. Keiko backed to the opposite wall until

Yôji wriggled after him.

Toad sat on the floor. He was perhaps three inches long and flat. His skin was cream-brown and covered with cream-brown pimples. "Ugh!" said Keiko. He had four big webbed feet and a wise look on his face; his cheeks went in and out as he puffed.

"He's hideous," said Keiko.

"He's beautiful," said Yôji. "Look at his eyes." Toad's eyes were big in his head, red gold and they shone.

"Where did you get him?"

"Great Grandfather gave him to me. He's Great Grandfather's pet. He lived in the greenhouse. Now he lives with me. He talks to me." Yôji stroked him with a finger. "When I go croak, he croaks back."

CROAK
CROAK

"I don't believe you."

"Croak, croak," went Yôji and sure enough Toad went, "Croak."

What kind of boy was this who piped and talked to a little bird and a toad? Keiko wondered, and she said, "They wouldn't talk to me."

"They would if you stayed quiet enough."

Keiko stayed as still as she could, then she tried to croak. "Cro-ak." It didn't sound like Yôji's but Toad croaked back and, "I like him," cried Keiko but then Toad took two steps on his big webbed feet and Keiko jumped almost out of her skin.

Toad at once went back behind the screen.

"You see," said Yôji. Then, "Here's Old Mother coming to let you out."

"She'll be cross," said Keiko but Old Mother said, "How *very* peculiar! I put one child in this room. Now there are two!" and she smiled; her face crinkled so that it seemed to smile all over.

* * * *

"There is a good story we could play with Toad," said Yôji.

Keiko was used to Toad now, he even sat on her hand. "Be careful not to squeeze him or he'll hop," Yôji had told her. Keiko held him so carefully she hardly breathed. "A beautiful story," Yôji went on. "Great Grandfather told it to me."

"How can you play a story?"

"You just play it," Yôji said dreamily. "You'll be a kind princess."

"A *kind* princess?" Keiko was remembering the bump she had given Yôji, but he went on:

"One day in the palace garden..."

"What palace?" asked Keiko.

"Our garden can be the palace. You are playing with a golden ball."

"I haven't got a golden ball."

"You can use an orange. The ball falls into the palace pool and you cry."

"I wouldn't cry for that," Keiko objected.

"You must. It's in the story; 'Ripple ripple' goes the water, and Toad comes up. He says ..."

"He can't say. He croaks."

"He says it in croaks. He says he will bring you your golden ball but you must promise to kiss him."

"*Kiss Toad!* No!" Keiko was firm.

"You must. It's in the story."

"If I do, what happens?"

"Toad turns into a handsome prince, me," said Yôji.

* * * *

Keiko was a princess in a pale blue kimono patterned with cherry blossom. Old Mother had brought it out of her chest. "I used to wear it when I was a little girl." The obi, or sash, was cherry red and Keiko wore her best red shoes.

Yôji hid behind the bamboos beside the pool. He had Toad ready and now Keiko skimmed across the garden's old stones, her butterfly sleeves fluttering as she tossed her orange golden ball. Titmouse flitted behind her. Then, splash, the ball fell into the pool, ripples spread – Yôji

made them with his hand – and there was Toad on the edge. His cheeks went in and out as, "Croak," Yôji spoke for him – but Keiko really thought it was Toad speaking. "Noble princess – croak – I will get your golden ball – croak – but you must promise ..."

"Promise what?" Keiko asked as Yôji had told her to.

"Croak – before I give it to you – croak – you must kiss me."

"I promise."

Yôji's arm went into the pool and brought out the ball – it was another orange but Keiko did not know that. He put the ball by Toad's webbed front feet. Toad blinked.

"Thank you," said Keiko.

"Kiss him," hissed Yôji. "Silly. Pick him up."

Keiko picked Toad up and, though she gave a little shudder, she bent her head to kiss him. Perhaps Toad felt the shudder, or perhaps in her excitement Keiko squeezed him, but he gave a great hop out of her hand and fell with a thump on the stones of the garden. He lay splat on the stone quite still and, "He's dead," screamed Yôji. "You've killed him."

"Killed him?" cried poor Keiko. "I couldn't have killed him!"

As the children stood horror-struck, Toad pulled in his legs and big feet. His whole body puffed in and out, his eyes blazed. Then, as Keiko bent over him, ppf! There was a terrible smell as Toad squirted a kind of toad juice, greeny yellow.

"Augh! Augh!" Keiko shrank back.

"I'm glad," said Yôji. He was pale with

fury. "That's to show you how much he hates you and you'll never hold anything of mine again, not ever ..."

* * * *

Keiko ran into the kitchen to Old Mother.

"*Not* in the kitchen in your outdoor shoes," but Keiko could not stop for her shoes; she put her arms round Old Mother, holding to her tight and sobbed and sobbed. Old Mother waited then, as the sobs grew less, "What is it?" she asked. "Tell Old Mother."

"I never do anything right," cried Keiko. "I never *will* do anything right. I hurt things. Wah! Wah!" she cried again as she thought of poor Toad and sobbed, "Yôji's so cross but I can't help it. I can't."

"Of course you can. Weren't you a beautiful princess?" said Old Mother. "There are several things you could do very well. For instance, to make up to Toad and Yôji you could make them a pretend picnic. They'd like that."

The tears stopped. "How do you pretend a picnic?"

"Have it in the garden," said Old Mother. "A flat stone for a table. You could make it pretty with flowers and moss, maple leaves for red plates. You can cut up pine needles for chopsticks." Keiko's eyes began to shine. "But you'll need careful fingers," said Old Mother.

Keiko looked at her fingers doubtfully but it was a fine picnic. Gen-san went into the spinney and found her acorn cups for bowls. Old Mother showed her how to mix chalk with water to mould into rice cakes with dots of green grass.

More grass, chopped up, made seaweed; akana weed, chopped fine, made red rice; cut-up petals of a cream chrysanthemum made noodles; the pod fluffs of Old Mother's clematis made spun sugar cakes, while the berries of the creeper that grew beside the porch made beautiful apples. Old Mother brought some meal worms for Toad food and, "I'll give you some nuts and berries for Titmouse." She helped Keiko write tiny invitations.

"How pretty!" said Yôji and, "How clever. Come on, Toad." Titmouse came too and perched on a bush and took a nut from Yôji's hand. In case there was not enough food Old Mother brought out special red rice to match the akana weed and sliced egg omelette. Yôji played some

special piping on his pipe. It was a wonderful picnic but Yôji would not let Keiko hold Toad.

* * * *

It grew colder. Keiko and Yôji had to wear their padded jackets, woolly hats and mitts when they played.

It grew colder still. Then one morning they woke up to snow. There were no sounds; everything was stilled.

"Yes," said Great Grandfather, "when I took my morning walk everything was white and glistening. It was like fairyland."

"Oh, I wish I was your walking stick and could have come with you," said Yôji.

After breakfast Gen-san came with straw boots

44

he had made for the children, the straw so thick and cunningly plaited that it kept out the cold. "We wear them in the snow," explained Yôji.

"I don't, nobody wears those nowadays," said Keiko. She wore red plastic boots.

Gen-san set up a bird table for Old Mother who put out seeds, nuts, a coconut and berries. "Winter is hard on the birds," she said.

"Titmouse will come," Yôji was sure.

* * * *

Great Grandfather painted the snow as it lay on the plum blossom branches, on the lantern, the little bridge, the frozen pool. Toad was in his own pool in the greenhouse fast asleep.

Great Grandfather painted Gen-san pulling a

sledge of wood through the snow and Old Mother, a shawl over her head, going to feed the hens. He painted Yôji with the snowman he had made. "Why don't you paint me?" asked Keiko.

"You can't keep still."

"I can," and Keiko kept still – it seemed to her for hours. Great Grandfather painted her at dusk as she pretended to put the lit lamp into the stone lantern, her face lit by the flame, the snow lit too. "You know, little girl," said Great Grandfather, "this is, perhaps, the best picture I have ever painted. Thank you."

Keiko glowed.

* * * *

"If this is winter, I like it," said Keiko. Perhaps the best time was the evening after supper, when they were tired of snowballing and sledging. Old

Mother put a quilt over the firebox table, with its brazier of hot charcoal sunken in the floor so that they could sit on the cushions round it, the children's feet dangling, even their knees warm. Keiko leaned against Old Mother's softness but Yôji sat up, his eyes bright as Great Grandfather told them stories.

"I thought stories came out of a transistor," said Keiko.

"Not Great Grandfather's ones," said Yôji.

Great Grandfather's were certainly different. The one they liked best was Lady Moon.

"Nowadays," said Great Grandfather, "you say that in the moon there are two rabbits making rice-cakes but, when I was a little boy, we knew the moon as Lady Moon and that every month, when she was full and round, she made herself

ready to shine down on the earth. 'The people are expecting me,' she said, and sure enough, on our porch and every porch in cities and villages, on the mountains or by the sea, little tables were put where Lady Moon could see them, and set with tiny dumplings that looked like the moon, bubbly rice crisps, potato crisps, sweets, and a special vase of horsetail grass. There were bowls of tea or saké wine to drink. They were all for Lady Moon."

"But the children ate them," put in Yôji.

"Of course we ate them. The mothers drank the tea, the fathers drank the wine. But one night," said Great Grandfather, "it was August and hot – up in the sky, Mrs Rain grew jealous. 'Nobody does this for me,' she said. 'It's not fair. I live in the sky too,' and she swished her skirts

so angrily that the umbrellas that edged them opened and almost spilled over on earth because they were filled with water; Mrs Rain just caught them in time and only a few sparkling drops fell through the moonlight, but the people on earth looked up and each of them said, 'Wah! Rain in August? Not tonight I hope,' which made Mrs Rain angrier than ever.

"The Wind God came by, holding his bag of breezes and storms. 'I, too, live in the sky,' he said. 'Nobody sets tables for me.'

" 'No,' cried Mrs Rain. 'They don't want us. It's not fair!'

" 'It's certainly not fair.' The Wind God sat down on a cloud. 'Let's show them what we can do.' For a moment he let go of one end of his bag and a gust of wind swept through the sky and

shook the porches.

"'You mean, let's go and spoil it? Upset all those tables set for Lady Moon?' Mrs Rain cried in glee and, 'Ho! Ho! Ho!' the Wind God laughed as he picked up his bag.

"Lady Moon had just come out and was sitting in the sky like a flower, smiling down on earth. When she saw angry Mrs Rain and the Wind God, she hid behind a cloud. There came a swirl of rain; Mrs Rain had swished her skirts so hard that all the umbrellas opened, rain fell in torrents, while the Wind God opened his bag wide; all the winds came out and blew with bangs of thunder. 'Ho! Ho! Ho!' laughed the Wind God.

"But what had happened? As soon as the first drops fell, as soon as there had been that gust of

wind, the people – old people, young people, boys and girls and babies – had picked up their tables, gone inside and closed their doors. Mrs Rain and the Wind God howled and hissed; he brought out his best lightning like fireworks. He and Mrs Rain shrieked but all the porches stayed empty, all the doors were closed. There was nothing left for Mrs Rain and the Wind God to do but go home.

"When they had gone, Lady Moon came out from behind her cloud. She could have cried when she saw the empty porches, the closed doors, but, 'Never mind,' she said. 'Even though there's no-one to see I will do my duty and shine.' She shone over all the earth.

"And what happened then? The doors were opened, the people came out on the porches,

the tiny tables were set out again and songs of welcome floated up to her. 'Lady Moon, Lady Moon, you are always more beautiful after wind and rain. Welcome. Welcome.'"

That was the end of the story but, "Could we make a table here for Lady Moon?" asked Yôji.

"It's not the Moon Festival but we'll do it next time she's full," promised Old Mother.

* * * *

On the porch under the full moon it was so cold the children had to wear their outdoor clothes though Gen-san had lit a brazier of hot coals. The tiny table was set with all the good things Great Grandfather had told of. Old Mother had brought out the doll bowls and dishes she had had as a child; they were patterned with plum blossom

and little people, the china so thin you could see through it. "Very precious," said Old Mother. "Please take great care. I trust you."

The moonlight glittered on the snow and made shadows. An owl cried, "Tu whit a whoo." Titmouse, with his "bii bii," came for crumbs. It was all beautiful until, "We could play Lady Moon," Yôji said. "You'll be Lady Moon."

"I'll be the Wind God and thunder." Keiko was entranced.

"You can't. The Wind God's a he."

"So what?"

"I'm the he," said Yôji. "You're a girl." And because he was excited, "*Girl!*" shouted Yôji. Keiko jumped up.

At the same moment, as if a cloud had burst, there was a sheet of rain. No-one had wanted to

Tu whit-a whoo

be Mrs Rain and perhaps she had opened her umbrellas in spite but the rain was frozen into hard white drops that stung. Keiko, half-blinded, leaned across to slap Yôji's face, leaned too hard and upset the table. What was left of the food was scattered and the precious little plum blossom bowls and dishes broke into pieces on the tiled porch floor.

"Keiko! What have you done?" cried Yôji and burst into tears for Old Mother's plum blossom bowls.

Keiko cried too. She wept and wept. "No-one will ever trust me again," she wept.

Old Mother was not cross but the children knew she was sad, yet she told Keiko, "I would give all my bowls, if it would make you a little more gentle and careful."

"I never will be," sobbed Keiko.

"You will. You are already – at times," Old Mother had to say. "Look how still and patient you were when Great Grandfather painted you. What a beautiful picnic you made. How quiet you are when he tells his stories." She made Keiko sit upright. "As for trust: tomorrow you will go and collect the eggs all by yourself and bring them back. You'll see, not one of them will be broken."

* * * *

Where's Yôji? Keiko had thought as she went to the henhouse. Yôji was always there; now, suddenly he wasn't, nor could she hear the sound of his pipe. Come to think of it, she hadn't seen him since breakfast when he had been worried.

"I haven't seen Titmouse for two days," he had said and, coming back, the eggs safely in the basket, I know, thought Keiko, Yôji's gone to look for Titmouse. "Yôji," she called. "Yôji." No answer. Everything was still. The maple tree did not sough – it had lost all its leaves – nor the bamboos ssrh. The stream was too frozen to gurgle; the hens and cock were all in the henhouse. "Yôji," she called. Still no answer. It was then that she saw something red in the deep snow away from the path. It was Yôji's wool cap but it was lying on the snow. Keiko set the basket down and plunged off the path.She had to battle her way, the snow came over her boots. "I'll never wear them again," she vowed. "I'll wear Gen-san's straw boots that fit tight," but she reached the red cap;

then, *"Yôji,"* she cried in terror.

He was lying by the bamboos on his back, one foot twisted under him, one hand open on the snow. His eyes were shut. He was quite still and his face was a queer blue colour.

Keiko reached him. She could have begun to cry, instead she seemed to know exactly what to do. She whipped off her coat which was warm and wrapped it round Yôji – he was so small she could lift him. She rubbed his hands – he was not wearing mitts – while, over her shoulder, she shouted, "Gen-san, Yôji's frozen. Gen-san, come quick. Please come. *Please.*"

* * * *

Though he was chopping wood, Gen-san heard her. He came with long strides over the snow and in a moment he was beside them, big and strong.

"Koria! Tai henda! Wah!" cried Gen-san. Carefully he straightened Yôji's leg – the ankle looked an odd shape – picked him up and carried him towards the house. "Don't you stay outside, Keiko-chan, without your coat," but Yôji's eyes had fluttered open, then grew wide with alarm. "K-Keiko," he stammered, he could hardly speak. "Titmouse. T-titmouse."

And looking down where Yôji's hand had opened, Keiko saw his pipe lying in the snow and beside it the little bird, frozen too.

"Titmouse," she breathed, "Titmouse. Yôji must have found you."

Titmouse did not move when she touched him; the bright eyes were dull, the tiny claws stiff, the feathers hard and frozen. You're dead, thought Keiko, quite dead, and she herself began

to shiver. Yôji had said she should not hold anything of his again - "Not ever." All the same, she picked Titmouse up, cradling him in her two hands like a warm cup; softly, very softly, slowly, very slowly, she blew on him with her warm breath, and as she held him she seemed to feel the smallest movement, small as a watch's tick and the sharp little beak opened. "Wah! Wah!" breathed Keiko and, going carefully, again slowly, step by step through the snow, she carried Titmouse into the kitchen.

Nobody was there. Though she could hear excited voices, and Great Grandfather telephoning, she stayed holding Titmouse in her hands towards the hot stove; she could hear her own heart beating as Titmouse, his life blood warming, opened one eye, his feathers stirred.

"Keiko!" Old Mother came in but, "Hush," whispered Keiko. "Look."

Old Mother came close and their heads close together, they watched.

The feathers were soft now; both beady eyes were open; soon Keiko felt a faint flutter in the wings, then another stronger flutter and, suddenly, with such quickness she nearly dropped him, Titmouse was perched on her first finger. As his claws clasped the finger, they heard a trill, not the usual, "Tsui bii bii," but, "Tsui siisi kala, sichipii." Titmouse was singing.

"Wah!" whispered Old Mother. "He's saying thank you," and, "Yôji must hear this, even if the doctor is coming."

Noiselessly, Great Grandfather carried Yôji in. Gen-san held the hurt ankle. They all listened,

Tsui siisi kala sichipii!

entranced, Yôji's eyes, for all his pain, like stars, and such happiness filled Keiko that, to her surprise, tears came into her eyes. Then she saw that Old Mother's and Yôji's eyes had tears too. You have them when you're happy! thought Keiko. I never knew that.

* * * *

"Carry Titmouse to the bird table," Old Mother told Keiko when they heard the doctor come and carefully, treading slowly, Keiko carried Titmouse and let him hop down among the seeds and nuts where he began to peck and peck.

"Famished," said Old Mother. "Now he will be well." As if he had heard, Titmouse opened his wings and flew.

"Don't go so far away," called Keiko and, as if

he understood, "Tsui bii bii," piped Titmouse, "Bii bii."

Yôji's ankle was sprained; the doctor bandaged it with a firm bandage. They all put him to bed, but in a few days he was hopping on one foot, no-one could hop faster than Yôji.

Best of all, "You are a brave sensible girl," Great Grandfather had said to Keiko. "You probably saved Yôji's life as well as Titmouse's. I'm proud of you."

"Proud of me?" Again came those happy tears.

* * * *

It was New Year. Gen-san brought three lucky pine trees to put on each side of the gate with lucky bamboo in them and stretched a string of red and white coloured papers between. The

alcove in the house had fresh early blossom with sprigs of pine; the whole house was polished and one of the village women came in to help Old Mother with the cooking. They made special food for the New Year, decorated dishes: mushroom, lobster and nuts: sushi, wild rice mixed with vegetables, nuts, beans, fish, shrimps and strings of fried eggs, rice boiled with chicken, soup to eat with the sushi. It would all be eaten cold, ready in lacquer boxes – there would be no cooking over the New Year. There was a traditional cake and biscuits; candy made from beans, chestnuts and flour – "Very sweet," said Old Mother.

"Many, many people will be coming to see Great Grandfather," Old Mother explained.

On New Year's Day, all day long people came to congratulate Great Grandfather; the children had to be there on their best manners. Yôji had a cushion but Keiko had to stand. Old Mother had made her a new kimono, deep purple with a pattern of vivid flowers; it had a pink obi. Yôji had a short black kimono with the family crest on the chest, sleeves and back, with wide striped trousers. "This is my great grandson, Yôji." "This is my great granddaughter, Keiko." Smile and bow. Smile and bow.

For Great Grandfather and Old Mother people brought cards and small gifts, a fan, a pretty hand towel, in fancy boxes tied with red and silver ribbons; for the children there were little paper bags of money.

It went on all day; Keiko and Yôji began to wish New Year had never been heard of but, in the evening, what was this? Great Grandfather was twinkling; Old Mother bubbling like her own rice pot. There were footsteps, first on the porch, then in the house, and in came four people in their outdoor clothes, smiling and laughing, holding out their hands.

"Mamma! Papa!" Keiko and Yôji cried together as they ran, he hopping, "Mamma! Papa!"

"Yes," laughed Keiko's Papa, "we have come to fetch you."

There was a silence, then Keiko said, "We don't want to be fetched. Not yet."

Of course they were fetched but first, "Is this Keiko?" asked her Papa and Mamma: a little girl who carefully carried round bowls of saké wine,

who helped Old Mother with the lacquer boxes, who did not clatter with her chopsticks and stood by Great Grandfather listening, not interrupting, who moved gracefully with small steps in her purple kimono.

"Old Mother, what have you done?" asked Papa.

"Not I," said Old Mother. "Keiko did it herself."

"It's too good to be true," said Papa.

* * * *

It was true but not quite; Keiko was still Keiko.

Next day it was time to say goodbye. The luggage was in the car; Gen-san had cleared a path from the house to the gate and heaped the snow into a great wet soft pile by the steps.

Goodbye to Gen-san. "Next time you come I

make you a big bamboo horse. Sayonara. Sayonara, Keiko-chan." Goodbye Old Mother, dear Old Mother. "Make sure Titmouse comes to the bird table." Goodbye Great Grandfather.

"Look after Toad till I come again," Yôji told him.

"I'll come too," cried Keiko, but now she could not wait.

"Come on," she cried and, forgetting Yôji's ankle, "come on, Yôji." She pulled him across the porch. The steps were wet and slippery. At the top she slipped and dragging Yôji after her, they both went head first into the pile of snow.

"Wah! Tai henda! Children!" cried Yôji's mother.

"Keiko! You'll hurt Yôji's ankle," cried Keiko's mother, and both together, "Your coats, your hair! Wah! They're soaked!"

"Oh, Keiko!" wailed her Mamma, "why do you have to push and rush!"

"They'll have to change," wailed Yôji's mother.

"They can't. We'll miss the ferry." The Papas were looking at their watches. "They'll have to come as they are."

"I'm not cold," said Yôji valiantly, but Keiko could see him shivering. She was filled with shame and it was a shamed little Keiko who got into the car.

Great Grandfather, though, gave her a twinkle and a pat as he shut the car door; Old Mother gave her encouraging nods and Gen-san was laughing.

It was too cold to stay outside and the last thing Keiko saw before the car started was the sight of Gen-san, Old Mother and Great

Grandfather going away. She knew where they were going: Great Grandfather in his flip-flop sandals with his walking stick for his morning walk; "chk chk chk," Old Mother calling as she went to feed her hens; Gen-san to chop even more wood for the stoves. Keiko felt a great pang, then found her face was wet with tears. She put her fingers up to hide them but, "Why, Keiko!" said Mamma.

"You see," Keiko sobbed, "I so like Great Grandfather's house."

Some bestselling Red Fox picture books

THE BIG ALFIE AND ANNIE ROSE STORYBOOK
by Shirley Hughes
OLD BEAR
by Jane Hissey
OI! GET OFF OUR TRAIN
by John Burningham
DON'T DO THAT!
by Tony Ross
NOT NOW, BERNARD
by David McKee
ALL JOIN IN
by Quentin Blake
THE WHALES' SONG
by Gary Blythe and Dyan Sheldon
JESUS' CHRISTMAS PARTY
by Nicholas Allan
THE PATCHWORK CAT
by Nicola Bayley and William Mayne
MATILDA
by Hilaire Belloc and Posy Simmonds
WILLY AND HUGH
by Anthony Browne
THE WINTER HEDGEHOG
by Ann and Reg Cartwright
A DARK, DARK TALE
by Ruth Brown
HARRY, THE DIRTY DOG
by Gene Zion and Margaret Bloy Graham
DR XARGLE'S BOOK OF EARTHLETS
by Jeanne Willis and Tony Ross
WHERE'S THE BABY?
by Pat Hutchins